First published in hardback in Great Britain
by William Collins Sons & Co. Ltd. in 1987
First published in Picture Lions in 1990
This edition published in 1999.
1 3 5 7 9 10 8 6 4 2
ISBN : 0 00 663604 7
Picture Lions is an imprint of the Children's Division,
part of HarperCollinsPublishers Ltd.
Text and illustrations
copyright © Blackbird Design P/L 1987

Printed and bound in Singapore by Imago

CRUSHER
is coming!

Bob Graham

Picture Lions
An Imprint of HarperCollins*Publishers*

Peter has just cleared his room.
He is giving all his stuffed animals
to his sister Claire,

because tough Crusher is coming
home after school tomorrow.

'Goodbye Peter, give me a kiss,' says his mum.
'Please don't kiss me this afternoon when
Crusher comes home, Mum . . .'

'. . . and keep Claire out of my room
when he's here, *please*.'

'Crusher has come straight from
football practice this afternoon.
This is my Mum . . .'

'. . . and my sister, Claire.'

'Just go straight through to my room, Crush,
there's heaps of interesting stuff in there.'

'Hi kid!'

'Would you like some fairy cakes and
tea, Basher?' says Peter's mum.
'*Crusher*, Mum, and I don't think he would.'

'Yes please,' says Crusher.

'Come on, Claire, out you go. I'm sure
Crusher has better things to do.
Want to try my *Raiders of the Universe*
video, Crush?'

'OK Pete, hang on a minute.'

'Hey Crusher, you don't *have* to.'

'I've got the whole set of *Captain Slaughter* comics to read in the tree house when you're ready Crusher.'

'Be right with you, Pete.'

'If you don't want to come up in the tree house we can go and buy some sweets at the shop.'

'Whatever you like, Pete. I'll just
finish up here.'

'Three Sugar Bombs, please.
What are you having, Crusher?'

'What would your sister like?'

'Thanks for buying her the ice cream.
I'm sorry we've been stuck with her
all afternoon.'

'Don't worry about it.'

'We'll walk with Crusher to the corner, Mum.'
'Thank you for the cakes and tea,' says Crusher.

'It's a pleasure, Cruncher, come again.'